First published in English copyright © 2001 Abbeville Press.
First published in French copyright © 1998 Editions Nathan, Paris (France). Translated by
Molly Stevens. All rights reserved under international copyright conventions. No part of
this book may be reproduced or utilized in any form or by any means, electronic or
mechanical, without permission in writing from the publisher. Inquiries should be
addressed to Abbeville Publishing Group, 22 Cortlandt Street, New York, NY 10007.
The text of this book was set in Journal Text. Printed and bound in France.

First edition
2 4 6 8 10 9 7 5 3 1

Library of Congress Card Number: 00-107674